For Christi and
her students — in and
Believe — in and within
the Wizard within!
use — You!
Rainbow wishes!
Barbara G. Hailey
Nov. 1996

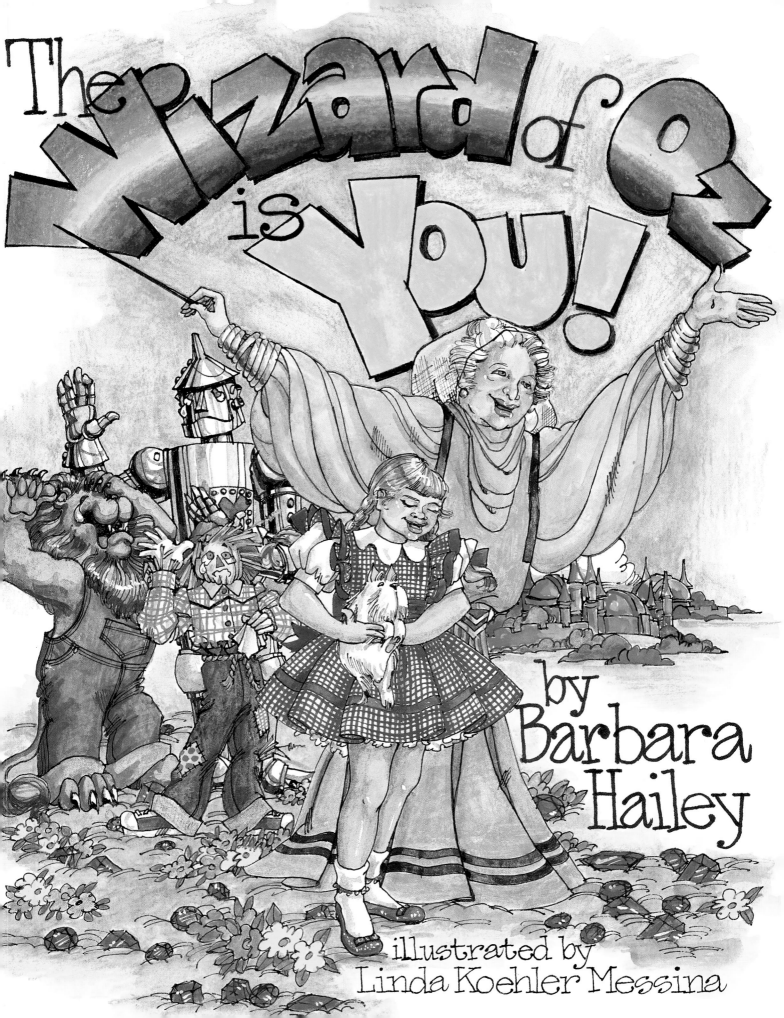

The Wizard of Oz is You!

by Barbara Hailey

illustrated by Linda Koehler Messina

The Wizard of Oz Is You

FIRST EDITION

Copyright (c) 1994
By The Southwest Theatre for Young People

Published in the United States of America
The Magic Unicorn Press
P.O. Box 345, Hunt, Texas 78024
210-238-4357

ISBN #1-882306-01-5

Library of Congress Catalog Card Number 94-077402

The Wizard of Oz Is You / By Barbara Hailey
Illustrations by Linda Messina

ISBN #1-882306-01-5 $24.95

Dedication

To Lillian "DeDe" Bushnell, my personal Good Witch, who shared this story with me...

All the prophets in heaven were gathered together trying to decide where to hide the secrets of life so that man would never find them. One of the prophets spoke up, "We will hide them far out in outerspace." But God said that man would go to the furthest corners of outerspace and would find the secrets of life. Another prophet suggested that the secrets be hidden deep in the ocean. God exclaimed, "Man would also go to the depths of the deepest ocean and he would find them." The prophets then questioned, "Where will we hide the secrets of life so that man can't find them?" God's loving voice replied, "We will hide them within Man himself — he will never look."

My sincere thanks to
Frances C. McCall, M.A., Linda Messina,
Steve Anderson, Pam Woodward,
Kathy Anderson, Mike Steer
and my devoted husband, Walter Hailey,
for their help in making
this "gift" for children of all ages
a reality.

I have a secret I want to tell you. It is a secret that only very wise people know, and since you are wise, it is time you should know that the real Wizard of Oz lives inside you. YES, it is TRUE!

There is a timelessness about the story of "The Wizard of Oz". This tale speaks to children of all ages who wonder how to handle their fears, meet their goals, how to make good choices and whom to choose for a guide

or mentor.

"The Wizard of Oz" is the story of Dorothy, who was a little girl. She lived on a farm in Kansas. She thought that life on the farm was very boring. She dreamed of a perfect world somewhere, somewhere over the rainbow.

Many people are like Dorothy. They feel unhappy where they are, and feel things would be better somewhere else. If they live in the country, they think things are dull. They dream of moving to the big city, where the action is, with lots of fun things to do. They think things would really work better for them in the city.

But someone else who grows up in the city, may live in fear of criminals, pollution, overcrowding, and dream of the country life, where people love their neighbors. The air is clean and everyone is happy and safe. And so it is that many people, just like Dorothy, dream of a better life in another house, another city or another place.

1. What would your world look like if you could make it just the way you wanted it?

2. My world would be...

One day Dorothy was hit on the head by a tornado (a really bad wind-storm) and she and her faithful dog, Toto, were transported to the land of Oz, the perfect place of which she had always dreamed.

She was welcomed by the Munchkins, the little people who lived there. They thanked her for freeing them from the evil power of the Wicked Witch of the East, who was killed when Dorothy's house accidentally fell on her. The Good Witch appeared and welcomed Dorothy.

But she hadn't been there very long when she met the

Wicked Witch of the West, who was mad at Dorothy for killing her sister, the Wicked Witch of the East.

1. How would you feel if you were Dorothy?

2. What person would you want to take with you to Oz? Why that person?

3. Are you afraid of the Munchkins?

Why? Why not?

4. Are you afraid   of the
Wicked Witch of the West?
Why? Why not?
Dorothy was afraid. But the
Good Witch stepped in to help Dorothy
by putting the ruby slippers
of the dead Wicked Witch of

the East onto Dorothy's feet. This was to protect her from the evil power of the Wicked Witch of the West. As the Wicked Witch of the West left, she said, "Just try to stay out of my way, just try. I'll get you, my pretty, and your little dog, too."

The wicked witches stand for the fears inside of everyone.

Fears of not being pretty enough. Or smart enough. Or brave enough. Fears of messing up and failing. Fears of not being liked by others. Fears can cause us to be afraid and shy of other people, or they can make us very nervous.

1. What are YOUR fears?

2. What are your wicked witches?

3. Is there one painful time that you felt afraid or nervous? What happened?

The good witch stands
for people in our lives who believe in
us, encourage us, and listen to us
carefully. They like us and think we
are great just the way we are.
They help us to believe in ourselves.
They are our mentors or teachers
who help us try tasks on our own.
They are happy for us when we

succeed. They could be coaches, parents, uncles, aunts, teachers, neighbors, or grandparents.

    1. Who are YOUR good witches?

    2. How do your good witches treat you?

    3. Do you ever tell them that you appreciate them?

    Dorothy began to think this land was not as wonderful as she had dreamed. She wanted to go home to her family and friends who loved her.

"I'd give anything to get out of Oz. Which is the way back to Kansas," Dorothy asked the Good Witch.

The only person the Good Witch knew who had the power to help Dorothy was the Wizard of Oz. The people of Oz thought the Wizard was very powerful. He was someone who could get things done and make things happen for them. He was someone they could depend upon to help them, rescue them, get them out of trouble.

Dorothy decided to find the Wizard, this magical person who could snap his fingers and transport her back home

We all have people in our lives we think are magical. We look up to them and respect them. If we could just get to them, we could learn what they know and get what we want. We may feel they have power over us to make us happy or sad. We may think of a parent or a coach who is like the Wizard for us.

1. Who are the wizards in your life?

2. What do you expect them to do for you?

Now, the Wizard lived in Emerald City in the Land of Oz and Dorothy could reach him by following the Yellow Brick Road. The Yellow Brick Road stands for the rules we must abide by to reach worthy goals, such as the Ten Commandments and the Golden Rule. They are rules we are familiar with: Always tell the truth. Don't cheat or steal. Share with others. Be a loyal friend. Respect others. Treat others like you want to be treated. Work hard and never, never, NEVER give up your dreams.

1. What are other good rules to live by?

2. What are the hardest rules for you to keep?

3. What happens when we don't live by the rules?

As Dorothy traveled down the Yellow Brick Road with her dog, Toto, the first person she met was the Scarecrow. The Scarecrow said he did not have a brain. She told him she was going to Oz to see the Wizard who would help her get home.

The Scarecrow asked, "Do you think if I went with you, the Wizard could give me a brain?"

"I couldn't say, but even if he didn't, you'd be no worse off than you are now," responded Dorothy.

So the Scarecrow joined Dorothy on her journey. Next, they met a Tin Man who said he did not have a heart. Dorothy and the Scarecrow oiled his rusty joints so he could move, and off they all went to meet the Wizard. The Wizard had all kinds of answers. Surely he could give the Tin Man a heart.

Then, they ran into a lion who had a big problem: he felt he did not have any courage. He hid his lack of courage by being mean.

"Don't you think the Wizard could help him, too," the Scarecrow asked Dorothy. "I don't see why not," exclaimed Dorothy to comfort the Lion. "The Wizard will fix everything!"

So along they went down the Yellow Brick Road. The four of them were becoming friends and they were finding strength and support in their friendship. Suddenly, the road turned and went through a very scary, spooky forest. The Wicked Witch was doing her best to scare them into quitting and forgetting their goals, giving up their dreams. But they were not frightened off by the threats of the Wicked Witch or her dangerous creatures. They chose to go on to ask the Wizard to grant their requests.

1. What are YOUR goals and dreams?
2. What would it take to make YOU give up your goals and dreams?
3. What would you ask the Wizard for?

The four found strength in their friendship. The Scarecrow, Tin Man, and the Lion vowed to help Dorothy get back home. Even if they didn't get their desires, they wanted their friend, Dorothy, to have her wish.

1. How do you know when a friend is a true friend?

2. Are you happy for YOUR friend when something nice happens?

At last they saw the Emerald City; they would finally meet the Wizard! As they got closer, they walked through a field of beautiful smelling flowers called poppies. But the poppies were very dangerous and lulled them to sleep with thoughts of waiting until later to reach their goals. Old fears returned; thoughts of not being good enough, smart enough, deserving enough, or tough enough to follow through and make their dreams come true. But then the Good Witch appeared and helped them get back onto the Yellow Brick Road, believe in themselves again and reach out for their dreams.

1. What things discourage you like the poppy patch did Dorothy and her friends?

2. What keeps YOU from being the best you can be?

3. Would you listen to suggestions from your Good Witch?

. Our good witches encourage us when we get down. Just as we yell for our favorite team, they cheer us on to find courage and strength to believe in ourselves again, then point our hearts and our minds toward our goal.

Finally, after following the long Yellow Brick Road, going through the scary forest and the poppies, they arrived in Oz.

The Emerald City where the Wizard lived, was like nothing they had ever seen.

One of the people in Oz even had a

horse that changed colors.

1. Do you know people who change color or personality from time to time?

2. What makes you feel a happy yellow, a sad purple or an angry red? They were all excited. At last their dreams would come true. But the Wizard told them he wasn't going to help them get what they wanted until they killed the Wicked Witch of the West and brought him her broom as proof that she was really dead.

The four of them set out to accomplish the task. Even though they were scared of the the fierce flying monkeys and the Witch's mean palace guards, they worked together to succeed.

1. Who or what scares you most? Why?
2. What is the best way to overcome those fears?

After they killed the Wicked Witch, they grabbed her broom and rushed back to the Wizard.
What did they discover when they met with the Wizard? The Wizard

was a fake. He did not perform magic. He was just a man, but a very wise man. There are very wise people in the world who can help us and teach us, but they can't work magic. They may show us **how** to conquer our fears and make better choices, but we must do it for ourselves. They can't do it for us.

We have to face our fears - face our wicked witches and find the courage within ourselves to destroy them before we can fulfill our dreams.

Each of Dorothy's friends had a particular request of the Wizard. The Scarecrow said he didn't have a brain. But he was the one who was always solving the problems along the way. The Scarecrow did have a brain, but he just didn't have any proof that he had a brain. So the wise Wizard gave him a diploma! Now he had proof of what he had all along. The cowardly Lion said he had no courage. But what is courage? Is it the lack of fear or is it the overcoming of fear? The Lion faced his fear of death when he saved his friend, Dorothy, from the power of the Wicked Witch. He demonstrated true courage by facing his fear and overcoming it. But, he had no proof. The Wizard presented him a medal of courage as evidence of his bravery.

1. What do YOU think courage is?

2. Whom do YOU think of when you think of a person that is brave?

3. Do YOU remember what you were going to ask the Wizard?

4. How will you know when you get it?

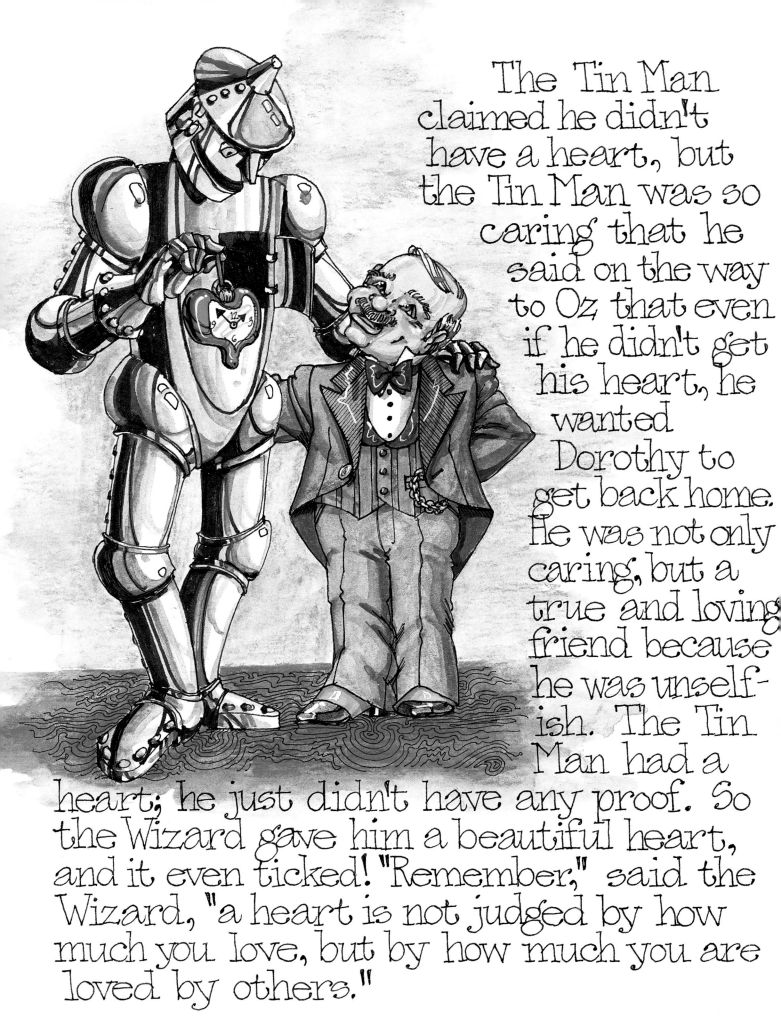

The Tin Man claimed he didn't have a heart, but the Tin Man was so caring that he said on the way to Oz that even if he didn't get his heart, he wanted Dorothy to get back home. He was not only caring, but a true and loving friend because he was unselfish. The Tin Man had a heart; he just didn't have any proof. So the Wizard gave him a beautiful heart, and it even ticked! "Remember," said the Wizard, "a heart is not judged by how much you love, but by how much you are loved by others."

As for Dorothy, she was going to go off in the balloon back to Kansas with the Wizard, but the balloon left without her. "Oh, no!" she cried. "Now I'll never get back to Aunt Em." She was very disappointed.

1. What do **YOU** do when you are disappointed?

2. Who or what disappoints you?

Dorothy was in tears. "Stay with us then, Dorothy," consoled the Lion. "We all love you. We don't want you to go." Suddenly they looked

up and whom did they see but the Good Witch. She comforted Dorothy and said, "You don't need to be helped any longer. You've always had the power to go back to Kansas."

"What have you learned Dorothy?" questioned the Scarecrow.

Dorothy replied, "If I ever go looking for my heart's desire again, I won't look any further than my own back yard. Because if it isn't there, I never really needed it anyway."

To reach our heart's desire takes three things:

1. The Knowledge to accomplish the things we want in life.

2. The ability to love and to be loved.

3. The courage to carry on through life's challenges and never give up our dreams. If we ever go looking for our hearts' desires, we needn't look any further than our own back yard. Where is that?

IT'S WITHIN YOURSELF.

The Scarecrow was angry with himself for not thinking of this for Dorothy. But the Good Witch explained, that Dorothy had to find it out for herself. Then and only then could Dorothy use the power of her magic slippers to transfer her back

home or wherever she wanted to go! "You had to discover the power of the ruby slippers for yourself.

I couldn't do it for you,"
explained the Good Witch.
The magic slippers stand
for the talent, the power that
we all have within us. Once we
have the courage to

use our talents, the
determination
to develop them
and faith
in ourselves,
they will
enrich our lives
and the lives
of those around us.
1. What is YOUR magic?
2. What are YOUR talents?
3. Are you starting to use them?

The message of the
Wizard of Oz is that the real
Wizard of Oz lives within you.
You must give yourself the
power to take control of your
thoughts, to overcome your
fears and follow the Yellow
Brick Road of rules to accomplish your dreams. No one
can do it for you!
So never forget!

The Wizard of Oz Is You!

To order copies of **"The Wizard of Oz Is You!"** for family and friends, just complete, detach and mail any one of the postage paid cards on the right. We are looking forward to hearing from you!

For teacher's guides and more information on other educational material for young people, contact:

The Magic Unicorn Press
P.O. Box 345
Hunt, Texas 78024
Phone: 210-238-4357
Fax: 210-238-4075

I'd like to order _____ copies of
"The Wizard of Oz Is You!"

SHIP TO:
Name:_____

Shipping Address: _____

City: _____ State: _____ Zip: _____

Daytime Phone (___) _____

$24.95 each book
$3.50 shipping and handling for every two copies

Credit Card (Circle one):   VISA   MC   AMEX
Credit Card Number: _____
Signature on Card: _____

I'd like to order _____ copies of
"The Wizard of Oz Is You!"

SHIP TO:
Name:_____

Shipping Address: _____

City: _____ State: _____ Zip: _____

Daytime Phone (___) _____

$24.95 each book
$3.50 shipping and handling for every two copies

Credit Card (Circle one):   VISA   MC   AMEX
Credit Card Number: _____
Signature on Card: _____

I'd like to order _____ copies of
"The Wizard of Oz Is You!"

SHIP TO:
Name:_____

Shipping Address: _____

City: _____ State: _____ Zip: _____

Daytime Phone (___) _____

$24.95 each book
$3.50 shipping and handling for every two copies

Credit Card (Circle one):   VISA   MC   AMEX
Credit Card Number: _____
Signature on Card: _____

BUSINESS REPLY MAIL
FIRST CLASS   PERMIT NO. 300   HUNT, TEXAS

POSTAGE WILL BE PAID BY ADDRESSEE

THE MAGIC UNICORN PRESS
P.O. BOX 345
HUNT, TEXAS 78024

BUSINESS REPLY MAIL
FIRST CLASS   PERMIT NO. 300   HUNT, TEXAS

POSTAGE WILL BE PAID BY ADDRESSEE

THE MAGIC UNICORN PRESS
P.O. BOX 345
HUNT, TEXAS 78024

BUSINESS REPLY MAIL
FIRST CLASS   PERMIT NO. 300   HUNT, TEXAS

POSTAGE WILL BE PAID BY ADDRESSEE

THE MAGIC UNICORN PRESS
P.O. BOX 345
HUNT, TEXAS 78024

The Wizard
of Oz
Is You!

To order copies of **"The Wizard of Oz Is You!"** for family and friends, just complete, detach and mail any one of the postage paid cards on the right. We are looking forward to hearing from you!

For teacher's guides and more information on other educational material for young people, contact:

The Magic Unicorn Press
P.O. Box 345
Hunt, Texas 78024
Phone: 210-238-4357
Fax: 210-238-4075

I'd like to order _____ copies of
"The Wizard of Oz Is You!"

SHIP TO:
Name:_____
Shipping Address: _____
City: _____ State: _____ Zip: _____
Daytime Phone (___) _____

$24.95 each book
$3.50 shipping and handling for every two copies

Credit Card (Circle one):   VISA   MC   AMEX
Credit Card Number: _____
Signature on Card: _____

I'd like to order _____ copies of
"The Wizard of Oz Is You!"

SHIP TO:
Name:_____
Shipping Address: _____
City: _____ State: _____ Zip: _____
Daytime Phone (___) _____

$24.95 each book
$3.50 shipping and handling for every two copies

Credit Card (Circle one):   VISA   MC   AMEX
Credit Card Number: _____
Signature on Card: _____

I'd like to order _____ copies of
"The Wizard of Oz Is You!"

SHIP TO:
Name:_____
Shipping Address: _____
City: _____ State: _____ Zip: _____
Daytime Phone (___) _____

$24.95 each book
$3.50 shipping and handling for every two copies

Credit Card (Circle one):   VISA   MC   AMEX
Credit Card Number: _____
Signature on Card:

BUSINESS REPLY MAIL

FIRST CLASS   PERMIT NO. 300   HUNT, TEXAS

POSTAGE WILL BE PAID BY ADDRESSEE

THE MAGIC UNICORN PRESS
P.O. BOX 345
HUNT, TEXAS 78024

BUSINESS REPLY MAIL

FIRST CLASS   PERMIT NO. 300   HUNT, TEXAS

POSTAGE WILL BE PAID BY ADDRESSEE

THE MAGIC UNICORN PRESS
P.O. BOX 345
HUNT, TEXAS 78024

BUSINESS REPLY MAIL

FIRST CLASS   PERMIT NO. 300   HUNT, TEXAS

POSTAGE WILL BE PAID BY ADDRESSEE

THE MAGIC UNICORN PRESS
P.O. BOX 345
HUNT, TEXAS 78024